To William, with
best wishes.

Don Worcester
May 23, 1990

WAR PONY

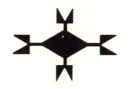

WAR PONY

By Donald Worcester

Illustrations by Paige Pauley

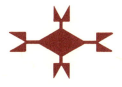

A SUNDANCE BOOK

Texas Christian University Press · Fort Worth

Copyright © 1961 and 1984 by Donald Worcester
First published by Henry Z. Walck, Inc.

Illustrations ©1984 by Paige Pauley

Library of Congress Cataloging in Publication Data

Worcester, Donald Emmet, 1915–
  War pony.

  Summary: A pony from a Spanish ranch in New Mexico
is stolen or won by several Indian tribes and has many
adventures throughout the West before he finally returns
to the ranch.

  1. Horses—Juvenile fiction. 2. Indians of North
America—Juvenile fiction. [1. Horses—Fiction.
2. Indians of North America—Fiction. 3. West (U.S.)—
Fiction] I. Pauley, Paige, ill. II. Title.

PZ10.3.W923War   1984   [Fic]   83-40486
ISBN 0-912646-85-3

Design by Barbara Jezek
WHITEHEAD & WHITEHEAD

CONTENTS

For Melanie and Jonas

I

GAVILÁN—THE HAWK

THE YEAR WAS 1800, and the Spanish province of New Mexico was as troubled as ever by the horse-stealing raids of enemy Indians. From the deserts and mountains came the fierce Apaches and Navahos, who had plagued the Spaniards since the founding of Santa Fe, two centuries earlier. From the Great Basin to the north came the warlike Utes, to run off herds of horses and sheep. But most feared of all were the stocky Comanches from the Great Plains, the greatest warriors and horsemen of all. Like the other tribes, the Comanches had learned that the best horses were those raised on New Mexico cattle ranches, such as the swift cow ponies of the Sombrero Ranch, two days' ride east of Santa Fe.

Vaqueros of the Sombrero Ranch rode the open range every day, turning back stray cattle and watching for signs of Indian raiders. There were no fences anywhere on the ranch, except those of the ranch corrals. Though the cattle might stray and wander from one range to another, the horses would never leave the range where they were born unless driven.

There were several horse herds on the ranch, the *remuda* of saddle horses, the *manada* of mares and colts guarded by a powerful buckskin stallion, and smaller herds of yearlings and two-year-olds which belonged in neither of these herds. The horses roamed freely among the saguaro cactus and thorny mesquite trees, cropping the short, rich grass and finding shade under the cottonwoods and alders and willows near the springs and water holes.

A light bay mare picked her way carefully through the mesquite to rejoin the herd of mares and colts. At her side, awkward and unsteady on his long, angular legs, trotted a dark-colored colt only three days old. His mane and tail, and his legs from his knees to his hoofs, were of solid black. On his face was a wide, white blaze.

The buckskin stallion, his golden coat gleaming in the early morning sun, whinnied softly as the mare approached. He trotted toward her, the hard ground shaking under his black hoofs. The colt sniffed cautiously at the stallion, but he ignored it, touching noses with the mare and then trotting back to the herd. He ignored all of the colts, unless they were in some danger, until they were nearly fully grown, when he drove them away.

Other colts came to inspect the new arrival, and soon he was playing with them, venturing farther and farther from the bay mare's side. At her whinny he suddenly realized how far from safety he had strayed, and with a squeal of fright galloped back to her.

Spring passed into summer, and the colt's legs grew strong. He galloped about the Sombrero range, frisking with the other colts. As the herd wandered from place to place he came to know every part of the ranch, to enjoy the taste of bunch grass and the sweet smell of the air after a thundershower. Cattle shared the same range, and colts and calves often met and examined each other, sniffing and nibbling before galloping back to their mothers, tails high in the air, as if prairie wolves were after them.

Winter came, and a light snow fell on the New Mexico desert. The colt's hair had grown long and shaggy, and the cold air did not bother him. He nibbled at the strange, odorless blanket of white, then kicked up his heels and raced madly around the mare. At night he listened to the shrill yip-yip-yip of hungry coyotes and snuggled closer to the bay mare's side, enjoying the warmth and comfort of her presence.

With spring the grass turned green once more, and the colt's shaggy winter hair fell off in patches. As he shed his winter coat, he became a bright golden buckskin, like the stallion guarding the herd. His mane and tail, and his legs below his knees, were still of solid black, contrasting sharply with the shining yellow of his body. Only the white blaze on his face remained as before.

One day riders appeared, vaqueros of the Sombrero Ranch. They drove the herd into a huge corral. The colts stood close to their mothers, but one by one they were roped and thrown to the ground. While the mares whin-

3

nied anxiously, vaqueros placed hot irons against the colts' left hips. The sharp smell of burning hair hung over the branding corral. When the colts arose, the hat-shaped Sombrero brand was on them for life.

When the rawhide riatas were removed from his neck and forelegs, the colt leaped to his feet and ran to the mare. A man and a boy sat on the top rail of the corral fence, watching.

"What do you think of that one, my son?" the man asked.

"He'll be like the buckskin stallion. I think he's the best yearling I've seen this year. He has eyes as sharp as a hawk's."

"You're right. If he turns out as good as the stallion, he's yours. You can ride him a few years, then start a herd of your own with him. Watch him the next year or two, and see how he looks then."

"Now let them out," he called to the vaqueros. They opened the gate, and the horses galloped out to the freedom of the open range.

By late spring black hair had grown over the brand on the yearling's hip. One day the bay mare mysteriously disappeared. The yearling whinnied anxiously for her, but could not find her. She returned a few days later with a newborn colt by her side. When the buckskin yearling approached her, she laid back her ears and drove him away. He whinnied after her, but she ignored him.

As he grazed with the other yearlings, the buckskin soon forgot the bay mare. He grew taller and more muscular, looking every day more and more like the stallion.

The boy and his father, sitting quietly on their horses, watched him occasionally.

"He's the only one that notices us," said the boy. "He's a *gavilán*, a real sparrow hawk. That's what I'll call him— Gavilán."

By the time Gavilán was a two-year-old, he no longer grazed with the *manada* of mares and colts, for the stallion had driven all of the larger colts away. For a time they followed the herd, keeping at a safe distance from the powerful stallion. If they wandered too near, he laid back his ears, bared his teeth, and dashed at them, tearing up the ground in his furious charge. Finally the two-year-olds stopped following the herd, and wandered about the range by themselves.

Riders passed them frequently, when rounding up the young colts for branding or when returning strayed cattle to the range. The young horses were accustomed to seeing riders, and did not fear them.

When Gavilán and the others were three-year-olds, a group of vaqueros rode past them one day. The vaqueros circled around them. The only way open was toward the ranch corrals. The young horses raced ahead of the hard-riding vaqueros, who kept them from turning back toward the open range. Soon they were inside a high-barred corral, and a vaquero had leaped from his horse and closed the gate behind them. The young horses galloped madly around the corral, while the vaqueros watched through the fence.

"Calm yourselves, *chiquitos*," one of them said to the horses. "There's no place for you to go."

The boy and his father rode up to the corral. They slipped from their horses and let the reins fall to the ground. The well-trained cow ponies stood as if tied while father and son climbed the fence. The father looked carefully at the young horses as they milled about the corral.

"The buckskin and those three bays and the roan look strong enough," he said to the vaqueros. "Cut them out and start breaking them. Let the others run loose for another year. No use ruining good colts by riding them too young."

"*Sí*, Don Antonio," one of the vaqueros replied. With the help of other riders, he separated Gavilán and the four others. They opened the gate and let the remaining three-year-olds race away to the open range once more.

The vaqueros dismounted and walked into the corral, braided rawhide riatas in their hands. The young stallions milled and turned, but there was no escape. Riatas hissed through the air and settled over the roan's head. He plunged and fought the choking ropes, while another vaquero skillfully threw a loop around his front legs. In a moment he was on the ground, with a vaquero on his neck, holding his head down so he could not rise. A vaquero slipped the rawhide bozal or nosepiece of a hackamore over his nose and slipped the leather headstall behind his ears.

Gavilán was next. He had almost forgotten the choking rope that had held him easily when, as a young colt, he was branded. Squealing with rage he reared and plunged, but the ropes held. He fought until exhausted, then stood, legs wide apart, staring at the vaqueros.

9

They spoke to him in soothing tones, and worked him out of the corral and into another one. The boy and his father followed. In the bronco corral the vaqueros snubbed their riatas around a heavy post in the center. Gavilán plunged and fought once more, but they gradually pulled him closer to the snubbing post. He snorted with fright, his yellow coat turning dark with sweat.

One of the vaqueros walked slowly toward him. "Bronco, bronco," he said. "Easy, bronco. No one's going to hurt you." Gavilán trembled as the man placed his hand over the white blaze on his face, then petted his moist neck.

"When he's lead-broken and used to the saddle, turn him over to Alfredo," the father said to the vaqueros, gesturing toward his son. "The buckskin's to be his horse."

The vaqueros nodded. "*Sí*, Don Antonio," they said, and went on with their work.

One of them brought a saddle blanket into the corral and held it out for Gavilán to smell. The young stallion snorted and drew back, then reared as the vaquero tossed the blanket on his back. The man slowly picked up the blanket, and kept tossing it at Gavilán, over his back and under his legs, until the horse stood quietly, quivering a little, but no longer afraid.

"That's enough for today," said Don Antonio. "He's learning fast enough."

The vaqueros gently removed their riatas from around Gavilán's neck, and he backed away. He stood with the roan while the vaqueros went through the same procedure with the three bays. The boy, Alfredo, brought a hatful of Indian corn and pushed it through the bars to Gavilán.

On the days following, the vaqueros continued working patiently with the young stallions, snubbing them to the post in the center of the corral until they learned not to fight the rope. Tirelessly they tossed the saddle blanket at the horses, until they no longer flinched or tried to break away. Finally the horses were so used to the ropes that they followed when the vaqueros tried to lead them.

"They're all lead-broken now," Alfredo said to his father. "It won't be long before they're broken to the saddle. I can hardly wait."

One of the vaqueros dragged a saddle into the corral and placed it on the ground in front of Gavilán. Gavilán sniffed of the leather and raised his head. Another vaquero placed the blanket on his back and smoothed out the wrinkles.

Gently he placed the saddle on Gavilán's quivering back. The stirrups fell to his sides, and he started to rear. The vaquero spoke to him softly and held him down. The other man reached under his belly and caught the cinch.

Once more Gavilán tried to rear, as he felt the strange cinch drawing tight, and again the vaquero held him. The man led him around the corral until he stopped flinching whenever the stirrups struck his sides. Then the vaquero pulled on the stirrups and took hold of the saddle horn, pushing and pulling to accustom Gavilán to the feeling of a saddle on his back.

For several days the process was repeated, until Gavilán no longer moved when the saddle was thrown on his back and the cinch pulled tight. A vaquero placed a hackamore on his head, slipping the bozal easily over his nose and sliding the strap behind his ears. The vaquero led him around the corral, and he followed easily.

"Time to ride him," the vaquero said. "I think he won't even buck."

Another vaquero held Gavilán's head while the first man gently placed his foot in the stirrup. Gavilán felt the pull on the stirrup for a moment, then the weight of the rider on his back. The horsehair reins tightened. The vaquero holding his head stepped back and climbed the corral fence.

Squealing with surprise and rage, Gavilán shot into the air, landing hard. He plunged about the corral, twisting and turning, but still the man stayed in the saddle, speaking softly to him. Finally the rider pulled Gavilán's head up and patted his neck. He rode the weary horse around the corral, pulling his head to left or right with the horsehair reins.

The other vaquero walked quietly up to Gavilán and seized the reins. The rider slid to the ground, while Gavilán tried to sidle away to the right. The vaquero mounted and dismounted again and again until Gavilán stood perfectly still.

Each day the vaquero rode Gavilán in the corral, teaching him to turn either way, to stop when the reins were pulled, and to stand quietly while a rider mounted or dismounted. One day he called to another of the vaqueros.

"Open the gate. We're going out."

The gate swung open, and the rider turned Gavilán's head toward it. Freedom! Forgetting the rider on his back, Gavilán raced through the open gate toward the range he loved, his black hoofs pounding the hard ground. He remembered the rider only when he was pulled sliding to a stop.

The vaquero turned him back toward the corral. For a moment Gavilán trembled with disappointment; then he obeyed the rider's commands and loped back to the corral.

The vaquero put Alfredo's bridle on Gavilán and rode him around the ranch for several days. Gavilán soon forgot about the open range and seemed to enjoy racing after the wild cattle. As long as he was on the ranch, it did not matter that he carried a rider on his back. One day the vaquero rode up to Alfredo and Don Antonio and swung to the ground. He handed the thin leather reins to Alfredo and touched his wide-brimmed sombrero with his forefinger.

"Here is your horse," he said. "Now he needs only to be trained to handle cattle. You will be surprised how quickly he learns."

Don Antonio mounted his horse, while Alfredo swung into the saddle on Gavilán's back. Eyes sparkling with pleasure, he rode at his father's side. They went far into the rangeland, while Don Antonio watched to see how Gavilán behaved.

"Ride him a little every day," he said. "Remember he is

only a three-year-old, so don't wear him out. Soon we will try him around cattle, and by next year you can use him in the roundup."

Alfredo rode Gavilán every day. He whirled his rawhide riata, and threw the loop over Gavilán's head until the buckskin stallion had lost his fear of the rope. He helped the vaqueros hunt for strayed steers, and rode hard in driving the unwilling animals back to their own range. Gavilán was a natural cow pony. When a wild steer broke from the herd and dashed for the rough country, Gavilán laid back his ears and sprinted after it. Nipping at its flanks, he drove it back into the herd.

Like many of the best cow ponies, Gavilán seemed to enjoy handling cattle. He came to know instinctively what his rider wanted him to do, and he stopped and turned so quickly Alfredo had to grip his sides tightly to keep his seat. Gavilán knew his rider so well that he could sense by the way Alfredo saddled him when there would be excitement. At such times he could hardly stand still while Alfredo mounted, but danced in place until Alfredo was in the saddle and then started off at a gallop.

By the time Gavilán was a four-year-old, he was a perfect cow pony, wise in the ways of cattle. He could outrun the fleetest steer with ease, and he never appeared to tire on long rides. When he was turned loose to rest for a few days, he often stayed near the ranch house, watching for Alfredo to appear. When he saw Alfredo step from the doorway of the ranch house, his piercing whinny echoed over the ranch.

One day Don Antonio and Alfredo left the ranch to ride to Santa Fe, capital of the Spanish province of New Mexico. They camped one night at a spring near the trail and reached Santa Fe in the afternoon of the second day.

They rode through the dusty street, past adobe houses, winding their way among the oxcarts and pack trains of burros and mules. Alfredo sat erectly in the saddle, proud of his horse, for he saw men stop to stare at the sleek buckskin.

In the plaza they tied the horses to hitching racks. Don Antonio greeted old friends and asked news of the latest happenings in Santa Fe, and of Mexico and Spain. The Navahos had been raiding ranches to the west. The Apaches made their usual thefts of horses, and the Utes came frequently from the north on their raids. Some renegade bands of Comanches had broken the treaty and run off what was left of the cavalry horses.

"Napoleon has taken Louisiana territory back from Spain," his friend told him. "Not only that. He promised never to part with it, then sold it to the United States. President Jefferson has already sent soldiers to see what it is he bought."

A cavalry troop rode into the plaza, returning from pursuit of Apache raiders. They had one captive, a sullen-faced young warrior, who sat his little pony stoically in spite of a wound. The soldiers' horses were weary and thin.

Don Antonio and his friend watched them, shaking their heads. "They can't even defend Santa Fe without good horses," the friend said. "For Indian fighting every soldier should have five good mounts, so some will al-ways be rested and ready for hard use. None of them has more than one, and some are on foot. Foot cavalry! No wonder we lose our herds."

"When are they getting fresh horses?" Don Antonio asked. "Have they sent word of their needs to Mexico City? Does the viceroy know? He should send them a herd from Durango."

The friend laughed, a dry, humorless laugh. "They'll get them soon enough. You'll see. The viceroy has or-dered every rancher to give them horses. Not nags he wants to be rid of, but the best he has. They'll take their choice. As soon as these men are rested they'll begin col-lecting them." He nodded toward the dusty soldiers.

The captain slid wearily from his horse and handed the reins to a soldier. He started to walk toward the com-mandant's office, when he saw the two Sombrero Ranch horses tied to the hitching rack. He stopped. Alfredo caught his breath. The captain was examining Gavilán, walking slowly around him, poking at his muscular thighs as if to test them. He glanced at the brand, then at Don Antonio, and walked on to make his report.

"I think he likes your horses—especially the buck-skin," said Don Antonio's friend, nudging him with his elbow. "You can say *adiós* to that horse. Good-by! Pretty soon, maybe, I think it will belong to the captain."

Alfredo stood as if frozen, for it seemed that the blood was running out of his veins. He was unable to speak, and for a moment thought he would be sick.

"It's not my horse to give away," said Don Antonio.

"It's my son's. They can have any of the others, but not that one." Alfredo felt better.

The friend chewed on a dry stick for a moment. "The viceroy's order said they were to choose the ones they want," he said. "What can you or I do about that?"

On the ride back to the ranch, Gavilán noticed Alfredo's moody silence. He kept on at a brisk running walk, occasionally cocking a black-tipped ear back at Alfredo, listening in vain for the sound of his voice.

At the ranch Alfredo turned Gavilán into the corral and fed him. Next morning he came to the corral at daybreak, saddled Gavilán, and rode far out onto the range. He stopped near a spring and let Gavilán graze, then rode aimlessly around the ranch. Occasionally he went to the top of a hill overlooking the ranch and corrals. He did not return home until after dark.

For three days Alfredo repeated these rides, ignoring the vaqueros who were bringing in wild steers. Perhaps the captain would forget about Gavilán. Perhaps he would see other horses which pleased him more. On the third day, as he rode to a hilltop overlooking the ranch house, he saw a group of horsemen approaching the corrals in a column of two's. They were cavalrymen from Santa Fe. Alfredo swung Gavilán about and rode to the far edge of the Sombrero range.

Late at night, when he returned to the ranch, he saw the cavalry horses in one of the corrals and heard the talk of the soldiers around their campfire. He hurried to the house. Don Antonio and the captain from Santa Fe sat there, talking. Don Antonio looked tired and sad.

"The captain is waiting for you, my son," he said. "He wants your horse for himself. I offered him two others in place of it, but he refused. He has an order from the viceroy, so there is nothing we can do." He shrugged his shoulders. "I'm sorry."

Alfredo tossed sleeplessly on his bed all night. At daybreak he watched the troopers ride off toward Sante Fe, driving the ten horses Don Antonio had given them. Among the horses he saw the shiny gold and black coat of Gavilán.

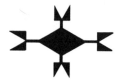

II

CAVALRY HORSE

AT THE CAVALRY BARRACKS of the presidio, the army post of Santa Fe, the new horses taken from the various ranches were divided among the soldiers. Each man now had five good mounts, and there was still a herd held in reserve. Training began at once. The captain saddled Gavilán, and rode at the head of the squadron. To the sound of the trumpet and to shouted commands they turned from a column to a battle line, charging across the parade ground with lances flashing. The well-trained cow ponies quickly learned the cavalry maneuvers.

The cavalry horses were guarded carefully. Herders watched them by day while they grazed, and sentries paced the area around the corrals at night. Gavilán often stood at the corral fence, his head over the top rail, looking in the direction of the far-off Sombrero Ranch.

One morning a rancher galloped up to the presidio and

shouted for the captain. Apaches had raided his ranch during the night and had driven off herds of cattle and horses. A bugle sounded assembly. In a few minutes the horses were saddled. The captain mounted Gavilán and, with the rancher at his side, led the way at a gallop.

The trail of the thieves was easy to follow, though it was already hours old. The troopers galloped along it, stopping occasionally to rest the sweating horses for a few minutes and to examine the tracks. All day they rode, and on into the night, as long as they could see the trail.

Gavilán smelled the smoke of burning sagebrush, and raised his head, his ears pointed forward. The captain halted the column, and sniffed the air. He sent Pueblo Indian scouts ahead. They soon returned and reported that the Apache camp was not far away. A few Apaches were guarding the cattle and horses, though most of the warriors were sleeping. They had roasted and eaten several steers, and had gorged themselves on the beef.

The captain made a temporary camp. The men loosened the cinches on their saddles, and squatted on the ground to eat *tortillas* and cold red beans from their saddlebags. The horses rested in place, putting their weight first on one hind leg and then on the other, hungrily clicking the rollers in their Mexican bits. With their reins down, they stood as if tied to the ground.

Shortly before dawn the captain gave orders. The men arose, tightened the cinches, and mounted. They swung into line and moved slowly and quietly into position around the Apache camp. As the first rays of the sun lighted the clouds overhead, the captain gave the signal. The troopers shouted and galloped their horses toward the camp.

A few of the soldiers drove off the herders and recaptured the herd before the surprised Apaches could scatter it. The captain and the others made for the main body of Apaches, who fled on foot. Gavilán raced after them, while saber and lance flashed. The skirmish was over in a few minutes. The Apaches who had not reached the rough country where the horses could not follow lay face down where they had fallen. The captain counted the slain warriors.

"Only three," he said. "That won't discourage them for long."

Herding the stolen animals back to the ranch from which they had come, the captain and his men spoke with pride. "Having good horses makes the difference," the captain told the rancher. "They never expected us to catch up with them so soon." He patted Gavilán's moist neck. "It was lucky for you we have such good horses now."

"You should have," the rancher replied. "Some of those horses were mine."

After returning the stolen animals to the ranch, the soldiers rode on to the presidio at Santa Fe. Gavilán and the other horses were lean from the long and exhausting run with no food and little water. The captain ordered the horses turned loose to graze under guard for a week or two, while they recovered strength.

The hungry horses snatched at the short grass and

gave no sign of wanting to stray. On the second day the guard tied his horse in the shade and lay down under a mesquite tree. Pulling his hat over his face, he fell asleep.

Gavilán ate the short grass until his stomach was full and his hunger gone. The other horses grazed nearby. Gavilán stood for a moment, head raised, listening to the horses cropping the dry grass. A rider passed by in the distance. Gavilán raised his head higher, staring at the distant horseman.

Gavilán looked at the grazing horses and then at the guard, still dozing in the mesquite tree's shade. He turned and walked away from the herd. Entering a ravine, he followed it until he was far from the herd. As he climbed out of it, he looked back. No one was following. He trotted off to his right, to swing wide around Santa Fe.

On the trail to the Sombrero Ranch, Gavilán kept up a running walk, his black hoofs clicking along over the loose stones. Toward sundown he heard other horses coming, and turned off the trail. Two vaqueros rode past. They checked their horses, and sat looking at him. One of them untied the thongs holding his riata to his saddle and shook out a loop. They talked some more, and the vaquero tied his rope to his saddle again, pushed his sombrero back on his head, and rode on. Gavilán followed the trail to the spring where Alfredo and Don Antonio had camped, and grazed there for most of the night. Coyotes yipped shrilly in the sagebrush, and desert owls hooted mournfully overhead. Gavilán stamped impatiently. At daybreak he trotted on toward the ranch.

It was nearly sundown when he galloped up to the ranch corrals, whinnying loudly. Alfredo stared at him from the doorway of the ranch house, scarcely believing his eyes. Then he ran to the corral, and did not stop until he had flung his arms around Gavilán's golden neck and buried his face in the black mane. Gavilán nickered softly, and nuzzled against Alfredo's back. He followed Alfredo to the corral and stood quietly while the youth ran to the saddle shed and returned with his sombrero

full of Indian corn. Gavilán ate it to the last kernel, snorted with satisfaction, and raised his head to look over the corral bars toward the old range. It was good to be home again.

Don Antonio came out to join his son. "I've known horses like him before," he said. "There are some, not many, that are like pigeons. Take them as far away as you want and turn them loose. They find their way home again. They can't help it. He is one of those horses. He'll never stay any place but here."

"But what about the captain?"

"The captain will have to realize it. He may as well accept another horse. Sooner or later Gavilán will come back to stay, for they will get tired of coming after him. But now they will come, and he'll have to go back. Another time, who knows?" Alfredo's smile faded.

Two days later the captain and three soldiers arrived. "I thought he'd be here," said the captain. "Two vaqueros saw him heading this way."

"My father says he will always come home," said Alfredo. "He says it would be better for you to take another horse instead of him." He waited hopefully while the captain threw his saddle on Gavilán's back.

"If you had another just like him I'd trade you," he replied. "Not just as swift or as tough. This horse is better than any Indian scout on the trail. He tells me when enemies are near. I need him."

Alfredo poked at the dirt with the toe of his boot, trying hard to think of something else to say, some words to convince the captain.

"There are some horses that won't live anywhere except where they were born," he said. "My father. . . ."

"I know," the captain interrupted. "I've heard of such horses. But he won't play tricks on me again. I'll see to that, don't you worry."

"He can never be cured of loving his home, *Señor Capitán*. It is in his heart. He can't help it."

"We'll see," replied the captain, trying hard to conceal his irritation, as he swung into the saddle. Spurring Gavilán savagely, he started toward Santa Fe on the dead run, leaving the soldiers to follow. As he rode he mumbled to himself. "Fool," he said. "You've made that boy think you'll mistreat his horse, just because you're afraid

of losing it to him. It's bad enough for him to lose it, without that." Gently he slowed Gavilán to a walk. Forcing himself, he turned and waved his sombrero at Alfredo. Then he faced the trail to Santa Fe, squared his shoulders, and rode on at a trot.

As he rode, he thought about Gavilán. Here was a real cavalry horse, the best one he'd ever ridden, the best one for Indian fighting. And it had to be one of those strange horses which could never be kept permanently away from its own range. One day it would slip away again, if not this year, then the next one, or the one after. Perhaps it would forget in time. The captain shrugged his shoulders. That wasn't likely, and he knew it.

He did not let the herders give Gavilán another chance to return to the ranch. Even when he rode his other horses after Indian raiders, he left strict orders to look after the buckskin horse well, orders which carried an obvious threat of punishment if they were disobeyed.

Once again he rode Gavilán in pursuit of Indians, for Navahos drove off a flock of sheep. The trail wound across the desert toward the northwest, through high-walled canyons with menacing cliffs on either side. Some of these canyons would make good places for an ambush. Which one would the Navahos choose? Nervously the soldiers glanced above and behind them, where Navaho enemies might appear at any moment.

The captain was calm, and he looked straight ahead over the horse's ears. He could afford to be calm even while riding into a possible trap. As long as he watched Gavilán's ears, he was sure the horse would warn him when Indians were near, and that would be time enough.

The trail led up the steep side of a mesa. It was narrow, and the sheer walls were rugged and high. A fall would be instantly fatal to man or horse. The captain held up his hand, and the column halted at the foot of the mesa. Gavilán's ears were pointing forward, and his head was held high, looking toward the top of the mesa. No one was in sight.

The captain, too, glanced toward the forbidding trail and raised his eyes to the mesa top. This must be where the Navahos had chosen to make a stand, to ambush the soldiers. This was where they were waiting, where they could not be reached. If the soldiers rode or walked up the trail, every man of them would be lost. He shrugged his shoulders in resignation. Of all the tribes which raided the ranches of New Mexico, the Navahos were the most troublesome. Their whole rugged land was a series of natural forts. On their high mesas they were impregnable. In battle they were not as fierce as the Comanches, but it was not often they could be brought to bay.

When the hiding Navahos saw the Spanish soldiers draw back from the trail they leaned their heads over the mesa rim, whooping and jeering, shouting the few Spanish words they knew in insult to the enemy. With their lances they pointed to the narrow trail, inviting the Spaniards to follow it. The soldiers tried to ignore them, and to keep their anger concealed.

While men and horses rested, the captain sent his Pueblo Indian scouts to search for Navaho cornfields.

They would burn any fields they found. This would not recover the stolen animals, but it was the only punishment possible. The Navahos might want for corn during the winter, but they would satisfy their hunger with mutton—Spanish mutton. There was little satisfaction for the captain in that.

The soldiers rode slowly back to the presidio, for there was nothing else to do. The captain was angry. If he led his men after Apaches or Utes, they might have to ride hard for five days, but in the end there was usually the satisfaction of punishing the enemy raiders, and of recovering at least part of the stolen animals. With the Navahos it was a different matter. He swore a terrible punishment to the next Indians who ran off herds from New Mexico.

For the next ten days Gavilán and the other horses rested and grazed, until they had fully recovered their strength. At noon one day a rider pulled up a tired pony at the presidio and hurried to see the commandant.

The rider was an Indian from Nambe village, northeast of Santa Fe. Comanches had stolen ponies from the village, he reported. The commandant frowned, for the Comanches had been peaceful lately, and he did not want to believe they had broken the peace.

"We have a treaty with the Comanches," he said. "They haven't broken it this year. A few young men are uncontrollable, but that's all. Maybe it was Mescalero or Jicarilla Apaches, or even Utes."

The Pueblo Indian shook his head. "Comanches," he

repeated. "Not many, but Comanches. Young warriors on a raid. They refuse to obey their chiefs."

The commandant called for the captain. "Go to Nambe," he ordered. "It may have been a band of renegade Comanches. If it was, find them and punish them, before they think they can raid us without punishment. You've been itching for a chance since the Navahos got away from you. Here it is. Now make the most of it."

Soon the captain was mounted on Gavilán, riding hard on the trail to Nambe. He was grim-faced, while the soldiers' faces showed only signs of fear or reluctance. The Comanches were the most numerous and dreaded of the wild tribes. The open plains where they lived, which Coronado long ago had called a sea of grass, were more mysterious and frightening than the mesas and canyons of the Navahos. With no familiar mountains on the horizon to serve as landmarks, men who did not know the llanos, the open plains, easily became lost. Then they wandered helplessly in circles until they died of thirst, or until they were killed by the Comanches. Only the ciboleros, the buffalo hunters, knew the llanos, and there was no time to find one of them to guide the soldiers.

At Nambe the chief showed the captain a wornout Comanche moccasin, which one of the raiders had left, and pointed to the trail. It led to the northeast, toward the open plains, where Comanches and buffaloes wandered at will. The captain led the way, followed by three Pueblo Indians who joined the troops as scouts, and by the soldiers.

They splashed through the shallow, muddy Pecos River and moved on. After the third day the trail was fresher. The Comanches had slowed down, as if they no longer feared pursuit, and were in no hurry to return to their own camp. The captain looked at the horses of his men, and at Gavilán. All the mounts had grown thin from the hard ride, but they had not slowed up, and they did not show any signs of breaking down. He pressed on.

They came to the edge of the Great Plains. The trail of the Comanche raiders was fresh now, only a few hours old. The Indians had stopped to rest their stolen ponies and to hunt as soon as they reached the edge of their own hunting grounds. No Pueblo Indian would dare to follow them onto the forbidding plains.

The Pueblo Indian scouts pulled up their wiry little ponies, and glanced uneasily from the captain to the emptiness ahead. The captain looked back at his men and their horses, then at the hesitant scouts. He pulled his hat down firmly on his head and spurred Gavilán forward.

Late in the afternoon they saw dust ahead, and knew it was raised by the Comanche raiders. Gavilán sniffed at the fresh pony tracks and raised his head, his ears pointing forward. The captain patted his neck.

"They're near, all right," he said. "But they don't know I'm after them."

He led the way more slowly now, keeping the dust cloud in sight. At night he ordered the troops into a sheltered draw by a small spring, and pointed to their camping ground.

He tied Gavilán where he could graze a little, and the soldiers tethered their weary mounts nearby. The Indian scouts moved a short distance away from the soldiers, holding their little desert ponies by long rawhide thongs.

One of the scouts approached the captain, and stood silently while the captain ate a *tortilla* and cold beans from his saddlebags.

"*Bueno*," said the captain looking up. "What is it?"

"*Señor Capitán*. It is not safe here. Let us turn back."

"Nonsense. They haven't seen us. We're safe enough till morning." He turned his back and drew a piece of dried beef from his saddlebags. The scout silently returned to his companions. Sitting motionless, the Indians watched the sun sink from sight and darkness settle over the area.

It was now dark. The captain stretched his aching muscles, arose, and yawned. He walked past where Gavilán grazed, stopping a moment to watch the horse eat. Then he went on to talk again with the Indian scouts. He strained his eyes in the darkness, looking in every direction. The scouts were gone.

"Turn back, captain," one of the soldiers pleaded with him when he returned. "Out here we're lost. They'll kill us for sure if they want to."

The captain shrugged his shoulders wearily, and dragged himself on to where his saddle lay. "*Bueno*," he said. "We failed this time. In the morning we'll start back. Now get some rest, all of you." He sighed heavily and stretched out on the ground, groaning with exhaustion.

Gavilán continued snatching at the short grass, while

the stars moved along on their course across the sky. A short distance away a coyote howled. He could hear the heavy breathing of the captain and his men, who lay exhausted on the ground. An owl hooted, and another owl replied across the little camp. Suddenly Gavilán caught a strange odor, and snorted loudly in warning to the captain. None of the soldiers awakened. A Comanche warrior stole out of the darkness, cut the tie rope, picked up the captain's saddle without disturbing him, and led Gavilán slowly away.

The Comanche warrior, when safely away from the soldier's camp, threw the saddle on Gavilán's back and slipped a loop of the rope around his lower jaw to serve as a bridle. He leaped to the buckskin's back and guided him to the Comanche camp, where four young warriors awaited him.

One of them was angry. "It was one thing to take po-

nies from Nambe," he said. "No one will be very angry about that. But you took a horse from one of the soldiers. We have a treaty with them. This will mean trouble."

"Not just one of the horses," the warrior replied. "I took the best one." He rode on into Comanche country. The others mounted and followed him. When it was almost morning they stopped to rest. By now they were more than half a day's ride away from the captain and the soldiers.

For three days they rode steadily over the open prairies, over hills and through ravines. In the distance they passed herds of buffaloes and wild horses. Flocks of antelope grazed on the prairies. Their sentinels saw the riders, and flashed their white rumps in the sun in warning to the others. In a moment the antelope raced swiftly away.

Late on the third day they reached the main Coman-

che camp. Conical tepees of yellowing buffalo hide were scattered in a great circle. Herds of ponies grazed in every direction around the camp. Most of them were small and lean, like the ponies of the scouts from Nambe, but among them were hunters and war ponies. A few of these, like Gavilán, bore Spanish brands.

The Comanche chief, a short, powerful man, watched the raiders ride into camp. He looked at the stolen ponies, and at Gavilán, and shook his head. He was angry, he told the raiders, for they had broken the treaty with the Spaniards. After the fall hunt, when the Comanches went to Santa Fe to trade, the buckskin horse must be returned to his owner. That would show the Comanches' good faith, and prevent the Spaniards from trying to gain revenge.

Gavilán, thin and exhausted from the steady ride, was turned loose to graze with other horses. A Comanche boy, mounted on a little bay pony, stayed with them until sundown, watching them graze, and turning them back when they started to stray.

At dark the Comanche boy drove the horses into the huge camp. The warrior who had taken Gavilán tied him to a heavy stake near a tepee. Other buffalo and war ponies were tied nearby. Wearily Gavilán looked in the direction of New Mexico and the Sombrero Ranch. He pulled against the rawhide rope, but it was strong.

III

COMANCHE PONY

AFTER A FEW WEEKS OF GRAZING on the rich buffalo grass, Gavilán was round of flesh and strong once more. Twisted Horn, the Comanche warrior who now owned him, begin training him for hunting buffaloes. At the ranch Alfredo had taught him to follow cattle closely so they could be roped. The captain had taught him the turns and battle lines and charges of the cavalry. Hunting buffaloes was much like roping cattle, for he had to race in close so his rider could discharge his arrows from only a few strides away.

Gavilán learned quickly what Twisted Horn wanted him to do. When they charged at a herd of buffaloes, he learned to pick out a fat young cow, and to race after her over the uneven prairie. He brought himself even with the cow on her right side, so Twisted Horn could pull his heavy bow and shoot an arrow to his left.

As soon as he heard the bowstring's hum and the thud of the arrow striking the cow, Gavilán leaped away, to avoid the slashing black horns. In a moment he was racing after another cow, and he continued this way until Twisted Horn drew him up, sides heaving, at the end of the hunt.

Gavilán learned hunting so quickly that Twisted Horn began training him for war. Riding at full speed he would lean down and pick an arrow from the ground. Gradually he began picking up larger objects. Finally, riding side by side with another warrior, the two of them picked a man from the ground and carried him away between them.

Twisted Horn was pleased. On Gavilán he would be

able to help rescue any friend who was wounded in battle, and for a warrior this was of first importance. Now he braided a horsehair rope into Gavilán's mane, making a loop around the pony's neck just in front of his shoulders. He cut a notch in the cantle of the captain's saddle.

By slipping his right arm through the loop and putting his left heel in the notch at the back of the saddle, Twisted Horn could hold himself flat against Gavilán's side. When Gavilán was accustomed to being ridden this way, Twisted Horn began shooting arrows under the pony's neck as he ran. Now he was ready to do battle with an enemy warrior, without exposing himself to enemy arrows.

"Why are you training him?" the chief asked Twisted Horn. "You must return him to the soldiers. You're just wasting your time."

"He's the best war pony I've ever seen," Twisted Horn replied. "You have only to show him what you want him to do, and he does it. He's swift, and he can run as long as any pony. I'll give the Spaniards five Kiowa ponies for him."

The chief shook his head. His people had made peace with the Spaniards, and except for occasional raids by unruly young men, like Twisted Horn and his companions, they had kept the peace. They needed to trade with the Spaniards, not to raid their herds. There were enough enemies whose ponies they could steal. Within easy reach were the Apaches, Navahos, Utes, Kiowas and Pawnees, and farther north were the Sioux.

The summer passed slowly. One day Twisted Horn mounted an ordinary pony and led Gavilán, to keep him fresh. He joined twenty other Comanche warriors, each leading his best war pony. As they rode, they spoke of the Pawnee war party the scouts had seen near the edge of Comanche hunting grounds.

All day they rode, camping for the night in a sheltered ravine. Before dawn they traveled on. It was nearly midday when they saw the Pawnee war party in the distance. Twisted Horn turned loose the pony he was riding, and sprang to Gavilán's back. The other warriors mounted their war ponies, and all raced toward the Pawnees. Gavilán laid his ears back along his neck and sprinted to the front of the galloping ponies.

The Pawnees drew up, brandishing their lances and shrieking their war cries. The Comanches circled around them, then pulled their ponies sliding to a stop. They counted the enemy war party. The two parties were nearly even. For a time the warriors merely sat on their restless ponies and watched each other. Then Twisted Horn loosened his rein and slipped his right arm through the loop of horse hair around Gavilán's neck.

Gavilán passed in front of the Pawnees at a steady lope, while Twisted Horn clung to his side, holding bow, arrows, lance and shield. Only one foot showed over Gavilán's back, and there was no target for the Pawnees. Twisted Horn waved his bow under Gavilán's neck and shouted his war cry.

Back and forth he rode between the two parties, until a Pawnee warrior, mounted on a black and white pinto, rode out to give battle. The two war ponies loped toward each other, while the warriors on both sides shouted encouragement. As the two ponies passed closely, almost brushing sides, the Pawnee warrior thrust his lance at Twisted Horn and accidentally gashed Gavilán's shoulder.

The two well-trained ponies wheeled and galloped back toward each other again. Blood flowed down Gavilán's shoulder and along his left foreleg. Twisted Horn saw the blood, and started to pull up and turn back to his own war party. But Gavilán would not be turned. As he neared the pinto he laid back his ears, bared his teeth, and threw his shoulder into the enemy pony with all his strength.

The pinto reeled from the unexpected shock, and the Pawnee warrior lost his grip and fell to the ground. Twisted Horn pulled himself quickly into his saddle. He struck the Pawnee across the shoulders with his lance as Gavilán wheeled about, then guided his pony after the riderless pinto. Catching the trailing rawhide rein, he led the pony to his own war party, while the Pawnee warrior ran to rejoin his companions.

The Comanches whooped loudly at Twisted Horn's feat. One of the Pawnees pulled the dismounted rider up behind him, and the Pawnees galloped away. Jeering loudly, the happy Comanches watched them go.

All the way back to the Comanche camp the warriors praised Twisted Horn and his war pony. Striking a live enemy in front of his own war party and taking his pony was more to be praised than killing several Pawnees, for it required greater courage and skill. Twisted Horn was now a famous warrior. Soon his name would be known to every Comanche band; and the Pawnees would never forget the warrior on the buckskin war pony.

The Comanche chief listened to the story Twisted Horn's companions told. It was good. Twisted Horn had been wrong to steal the pony from the soldiers, but his action against the Pawnees proved he was a real Comanche, brave and skillful.

"You must remember, my son," he told Twisted Horn, "from now on you are a marked man. The Pawnees will not rest until they are avenged. If they cannot kill you, they must steal our ponies, especially the buckskin one.

You must guard him carefully until we go to Santa Fe, when you will return him to the Spaniards."

Twisted Horn bathed the wound in Gavilán's shoulder and covered it with melted buffalo fat. During the days Gavilán grazed with other war ponies, under the alert eyes of a Comanche youth. At night he was tied to a stake near Twisted Horn's tepee. The wound healed and white hair covered the scar on his shoulder, contrasting with the black hair which grew over the brand on his hip, where the skin had not been broken.

From time to time the Comanches moved their camp, to find fresh herds of buffaloes to hunt. When they moved, the women quickly took down the buffalo-hide tepees. They tied the poles to the travois ponies, crossing

them over the ponies' shoulders so one end of each pole was near a pony's head while the other end dragged behind on the ground. To the dragging poles they tied bundles and baskets, behind the ponies' heels. In a few minutes every lodge was down, the ponies were packed, and the tribe was ready for the trail.

At such times Twisted Horn rode an ordinary pony and led Gavilán or the pinto taken from the Pawnees, so he would have a war pony fresh and ready for use if enemies appeared suddenly. He rode with other young warriors ahead or behind the women and children, ready to spring to his war pony's back and defend his tribe the moment danger appeared.

At the end of the summer the Comanches split up into smaller bands for the fall hunt. They spread out over the prairies to seek herds, for they must have dried meat for winter and robes to trade with the Spaniards in Santa Fe. Before the bands rode off, the chief spoke to Twisted Horn once more.

"Watch out for Pawnees," he warned. "They know we must divide the camp to hunt now. They haven't forgotten you. Don't enter their hunting grounds, for you may never return."

The band with which Twisted Horn rode moved far to the north without finding a herd of buffaloes. As they neared the edge of Pawnee hunting grounds, Twisted Horn grew uneasy. His companions noticed his concern.

"Are you afraid of the Pawnees?" one of them asked. "I thought your name was Twisted Horn. The Pawnees will go far away when they know you are near." Twisted Horn remained silent. Some of the young men were still jealous of his fame, and they could only enjoy his discomfort.

At the edge of the Comanche lands the band stopped and set up camp, while scouts rode out to search for a herd. A scout galloped into camp one afternoon, sliding his pony to a halt and swinging his bare arm to the north.

"There's a big herd there," he said, "nearly a day's ride away, in Pawnee country. It's the only one I saw."

The warriors squatted in a circle on the ground, and waited until the other scouts had returned. None of them had found a herd. They talked of the Pawnees, and of winter camp without food, and of the robes they needed to trade with the Spaniards. Twisted Horn said nothing, waiting for the others to decide. Was it more dangerous to face a winter with little food or to invade Pawnee country? They were Comanches, and he knew what their decision would be.

In the morning they broke camp and moved rapidly toward the herd. When camp was made at nightfall, the scouts reported that the herd was near enough to hunt in the morning. There were no signs of Pawnees in any direction.

At dawn the hunters set out, riding ordinary ponies as usual to keep the spirited buffalo ponies fresh for the tiring chase after the buffaloes. When scouts signaled that they were near the herd, they mounted the buffalo po-

43

nies. Twisted Horn leaped to Gavilán's back, holding his short, heavy bow in his left hand. The hunters divided into four groups, to dash at the herd from all sides.

Gavilán could hardly be held back until the signal to charge, when he raced into the startled herd. He carried Twisted Horn past cow after cow, waiting until he heard the thud of arrow into flesh before racing on.

44

When the hunt was over, the men quickly butchered the buffaloes and carried the dripping meat back to camp. The women hastily sliced it into thin strips and spread it out in the sun to dry. When the warriors had finished their tasks, they tied their ponies to stakes near the tepees and ate roasted tongue and liver and hump ribs until they could eat no more. Soon all slept soundly. Gavilán and the pinto and several other ponies stood where they were tied, shifting their weight from one hind leg to the other. From inside the tepee came the sound of

heavy breathing. In the distance coyotes and prairie wolves howled and snapped over the remains of the buffaloes. From nearer camp came the weird hooting of burrowing owls. It was like the night when Twisted Horn had slipped into the Spanish camp.

The next day the scouts reported another small herd moving toward the camp. Gavilán and the other buffalo ponies were tied where the grass was thick and allowed to rest all day. The women had all of the meat drying in the sun, turning from a rich red to black as it hardened. They bent over the fresh hides, scraping them tirelessly with flint knives.

Before slaughtering the second buffalo herd in Pawnee country the chief of the Comanche band sent his scouts far across the prairies searching for any sign that Pawnees had discovered them. The Comanches were more ready to flee than to fight, for, like all Plains tribes, they preferred to fight only in their own lands. None of them wanted to meet Pawnee warriors, but none of them would admit his fears to his companions.

No signs of enemies were found, and the chief ordered the hunt to begin. Twisted Horn again sent arrow after arrow into the fat, young cows. One cow turned from the milling herd and raced for the hills. Since he was nearest to her, Twisted Horn sent Gavilán galloping after her. One wounded or frightened animal would tell Pawnee scouts all they needed to know.

Gavilán sprinted after the swift cow. She crossed the first line of hills as he drew alongside, and Twisted Horn released his bowstring. As she fell, and as Gavilán slid to a stop and wheeled about, three Pawnee warriors galloped up and knocked the surprised Comanche to the ground. One of them was Bent Bow, the warrior who had lost the pinto in the battle with Twisted Horn. He seized Gavilán's rawhide rein, and they rode away at a gallop before Twisted Horn could shout to the scattered Comanche warriors.

The Pawnees rode hard all the rest of the day, until the ponies were covered with lather. Frequently they glanced over their shoulders, watching for angry Comanches, but none appeared.

At dark the Pawnees slowed the ponies to a walk, and rode on through the night. Bent Bow was happy. Since the day of his defeat he had thought of little except revenge. Now his honor had been restored. He had struck Twisted Horn and had taken his pony, a better one than the pinto he had lost.

It was nearly morning when they made camp. Gavilán and the other ponies grazed wearily where they were tied near the sleeping men. They had only a few hours of rest when the Pawnees arose. Bent Bow, Gavilán's new owner, tied a thin rawhide strand around the pony's lower jaw for a bridle, and leaped to his back. With a shout of glee he led the way toward the Pawnee village.

Late in the afternoon they reached the main Pawnee camp. The huts were solidly built, with grass roofs. Ponies grazed in every direction, for the Pawnees had huge herds. Here and there were some bearing Spanish brands which, like Gavilán's, belonged to Spanish ranches of New Mexico.

IV

THE WHITE ROBE

GAVILÁN REMAINED WITH THE PAWNEES during the winter. He grazed with other valuable war ponies. Bent Bow watched him carefully, although the Plains Indians rarely raided one another in the winter. The withered buffalo grass was poor feed, and the ponies grew thin.

At times when snow lay heavily on the prairie, Bent Bow brought strips of cottonwood bark to his buckskin pony. Gavilán stood staring across the white expanse toward New Mexico. He remembered the sunny rangeland where he had been born, the short, rich grass and the green mesquite trees. He remembered, too, the ranch house and, above all, Alfredo.

On days when there was no snow the ponies were turned loose to graze on the frozen grass. Pawnee boys, with their buffalo robes wrapped tightly around them, rode out from time to time to see that the valuable war and buffalo ponies did not stray too far from the village.

One morning when the air was crisp and cold and strangely quiet, the Pawnee boys came out only once to look at the horses. Gavilán turned away from the herd, crossed a small creek, and trotted south. The willows and alders growing along the banks of the creek shielded him from sight until he turned across the open plains toward his home in New Mexico, twenty days away to the southwest.

By dark he had left the Pawnee village far behind. He did not know it, but Bent Bow was riding hard on his trail, determined to find him. At night Gavilán stopped to rest and graze. He wanted to keep on, not stopping until he reached the ranch, but he was too weak. He snatched hungrily at the dry, tasteless grass.

During the night an icy wind arose, whistling through the ravines. By morning snow was beginning to fall, and the wind was still rising. Gavilán faced the wind for a moment, his eyes blinded by the driving snow. He could not go on. He found a sheltered ravine, where the wind came only in gusts. He stood with his back to the wind, waiting for the worst of the storm to strike.

The wind continued to rise, howling over the prairies, driving heavy snowflakes with the speed of Comanche arrows. The snow swirled into the draw where Gavilán stood, gradually rising in a soft layer over his black hoofs. Tremendous gusts of wind lashed his mane and tail about occasionally, and ruffled his shaggy coat.

Numbed with cold Gavilán stood with drooping head, while the snow drifted more and more deeply around him. There was nothing more that he could do to escape the blizzard.

A muffled cry came through the shrieking wind. Gavilán raised his head and turned to face the storm. He whinnied. In a moment Bent Bow staggered into the ravine and leaned weakly against Gavilán's shoulder. He flung his ice-caked robe over Gavilán's head and shoulders, and took shelter under it himself. Huddling together to share each other's warmth, warrior and war pony waited out the storm.

Snow fell all that day and night, but at dawn of the second day the icy air was clear. Sunlight gleamed in blinding brightness as Bent Bow led Gavilán through the drifted snow toward the Pawnee village. They passed the pony Bent Bow had worn out riding after Gavilán, but it was still too weak to follow them. All day they struggled, and it was late at night when they staggered into the village.

Bent Bow entered his lodge and fell exhausted on his robe. Pawnee women hurried out to Gavilán, carrying strips of cottonwood bark. While he ate, the women brushed the snow and ice from his back and covered him with a robe.

Gavilán did not have another chance to strike out for New Mexico. Bent Bow kept him tied securely each night, and the herders remained alert during the days. Often he stood looking across the empty plains, but if he tried to leave the herd, Pawnee boys drove him back.

When spring came, and the fresh green blades of grass

pushed their way up through the dark earth, Gavilán and the other ponies ate ravenously. Soon their lean backs were round with firm flesh, and they were strong again. Here and there where they grazed were the whitened bones of ponies which had not survived the cruel winter.

With spring came buffalo hunts and raids on enemy camps. Comanche raiders stole into the village. Twisted Horn and his companions risked their lives to get Gavilán once more, and to slip away with other good Pawnee ponies. But the Pawnees were alert, and even the skillful Comanches failed to reach the best ponies.

Sioux raiders, too, watched the Pawnee village, picking out the best ponies that grazed under guard, hoping to find them again while the Pawnees slept. Although they escaped with a few good buffalo ponies, Gavilán was too well guarded.

Pawnee raiding parties left the camp to raid these and other enemies, for stealing good ponies from enemy tribes was the great game of Plains warriors. On the plains a good war pony was likely to change owners many times, and a careless warrior could not expect to own a good pony for long.

A Kiowa party approached the Pawnee village one day, signaling to the scouts from a safe distance that they were peaceful. By the sign language of the plains they told the Pawnees that they wanted to trade for ponies. Their losses to Sioux raiders had been heavy, and they needed buffalo and war ponies so they could hunt and protect their women and children.

The Pawnees held council, and agreed to visit the Kiowa camp at the edge of their hunting grounds. All of the warriors who owned more ponies than they needed selected those they were willing to trade and herded them toward the meeting place.

Although he had no ponies to trade, Bent Bow rode with the others to help protect them from Comanches or other enemies. They made the journey safely, and found the Kiowas waiting.

The trade began. Kiowa warriors chose the ponies they wanted and began to bargain with the owners. They offered beaver skins, beautifully tanned elk hides, and short, powerful bows made from strips of the horns of mountain sheep, shaped and glued together. While the trading went on, Bent Bow sat on Gavilán and watched.

From time to time Kiowa warriors glanced at Gavilán, eying him hungrily. One of them, a man named Bear Claw, signaled to Bent Bow, offering to trade for the buckskin pony. Bent Bow shook his head, but the Kiowa warrior persisted.

Bear Claw spread his robe on the ground and placed on it a pile of his possessions. He looked up at Bent Bow. Bent Bow looked away. Bear Claw waited, walking around Gavilán, admiring the powerful muscles that rippled under the shiny coat.

Finally Bear Claw spoke to one of the Kiowa women. She hurried to his tepee, while the Kiowa warriors looked astonished and began protesting to Bear Claw. The woman returned with a large bundle in a rawhide, boxlike container. She placed it gently on the robe and stepped back. Bear Claw motioned to her to move farther away.

Bent Bow stared at the red and black and yellow drawings on the rawhide, while the warriors of both tribes

gathered around. What was in the container Bent Bow could not guess, but he could tell that it was some powerful charm, Bear Claw's good medicine. Bear Claw looked solemnly up at the sun, then slowly untied the buckskin thongs that held the bundle together. A mur-

mur of amazement ran through the Pawnees. Bear Claw drew out a white buffalo robe.

Bent Bow stared at the white robe, and looked at his companions. Kiowa warriors crowded more closely around Bear Claw, protesting angrily. White buffaloes were rare and sacred animals on the plains, and a white robe was the best medicine, the best guarantee of good fortune, that a warrior or a tribe could own. A man who owned one would rarely part with it for any reason, for few things except the greatest war ponies could equal its value.

While the Kiowas protested, the Pawnees pressed around Bent Bow. "Take the white robe," they told him. "With it your raids will never fail. You can steal many ponies from the Comanches. The Sioux will soon steal this pony from the Kiowas. One day you will steal him back from the Sioux."

Bent Bow still shook his head, but he could not take his eyes off the white robe. Few warriors had ever owned one. He would be famous among all the Pawnees. Soon he would have many ponies, instead of only two. He slid from Gavilán's back and handed the rawhide rein to Bear Claw.

Bear Claw swung to Gavilán's back without a word and galloped into the Kiowa camp. A howl of rage rose among the Kiowa warriors. The Pawnees quickly mounted their ponies and galloped toward their own hunting grounds, for the trading was now over. The Kiowa women began taking down the tepees. Soon the Kiowas were moving west.

Proud of his fine war pony, Bear Claw rode all along the line of Kiowas. The men frowned at him, nervously scanned the horizons for signs of enemies, and cast admiring glances at Gavilán. The white buffalo robe, they were sure, had brought good luck to the entire tribe. Now that it was gone they were plainly worried. Bear Claw had been rash. To trade his precious white robe was madness, no matter how good the buckskin war pony might prove to be.

V

▲▼▲▼▲▼▲▼▲▼▲▼▲▼▲

BEAR CLAW

BACK IN KIOWA COUNTRY Bear Claw waited impatiently until the scouts sighted a herd of buffalo half a day's ride from the camp. There were still not enough good buffalo ponies for all the Kiowa warriors, and none which could compare with Gavilán. Bear Claw rode his new pony a few times, so that each was accustomed to the other. Then he tied Gavilán where the grass was plentiful and let him rest.

While waiting for the scouts to find a herd for the hungry camp, Bear Claw polished his arrows, running them slowly through a grooved soapstone until they were straight and smooth. He smiled as he worked. When there were buffaloes to kill he, Bear Claw, would kill more than any other warrior had killed in one hunt as long as men could remember. His bow was strong and his pony was swift and sure.

A scout signaled from far out on the plains that a herd

was near. The chief swept his arm toward the buffalo ponies. The warriors mounted ordinary ponies and led the swift hunters. Gavilán tossed his head so that his black mane flew. The other ponies, too, sensed that the mad chase was soon to follow, and were impatient for it to begin.

The warriors divided into four groups and surrounded the herd. They dashed at the startled buffaloes from every side, turning them constantly in a circle until every animal had been slain. Gavilán raced into the herd, carrying his rider alongside cow after cow. Bear Claw pulled his bowstring until his arms ached. When the last buffalo fell and the thick dust began to settle, he had only one arrow left.

Proudly he rode among the slain buffaloes, giving away one after another to families which had no swift pony. The other warriors watched him, pride and envy mingled in their glances. Bear Claw's arrows were in more than twice as many buffaloes as those of any other warrior.

"Your pony is good," they told him, "for he has killed many buffaloes. He will be even better against enemies."

They did not say it, but Bear Claw knew that they had almost forgiven him for trading the white buffalo robe. Once he rode Gavilán in battles with enemy warriors, he was sure they would forget their anger and fears entirely. He knew also that he would not have long to wait. Sioux or Utes or some other enemy would soon appear. He kept Gavilán rested and ready, and watched for signs from the scouts.

A few days later Kiowa scouts sighted a war party of Utes which had come to the edge of Kiowa lands. The Utes were young warriors eager to win fame, reckless with their lives. A party of Kiowa warriors raced to meet them. Here was a chance for Bear Claw to show off his famous war pony, the pony worth a white robe.

The two war parties faced one another in typical Plains fashion. The chiefs hastily counted the number of enemy warriors. Neither side dared to begin a direct charge, for the numbers were fairly even, and neither had any advantage. Where the sides were of equal strength, many lives would be lost in a charge, and both camps would be in mourning for days after the battle.

For Plains warriors brave deeds brought greater fame than merely killing enemies. The purpose of the battles was to give the young men a chance to win fame by brave acts, to "count coup on the enemy," as they called it. Every warrior remembered each of his deeds or coups, and he recited them in a loud voice when his tribe gathered for any celebration, such as a Scalp Dance.

The chiefs, satisfied that the forces were equal enough to prevent a massacre of either side, sat on their war ponies and watched their young men perform. A Ute warrior on a stocky black pony rode back and forth between the two parties. Gavilán stamped impatiently and tossed his head as Bear Claw prepared to ride out and challenge the Ute. Before he was ready, however, another Kiowa loosened his rein and galloped out to give battle.

The two ponies circled and wheeled, darting in and out as the riders sought an advantage. The Utes shouted gleefully, for their man had struck first. The wounded Kiowa slumped over his pony's shoulders, while his friends helped him back to camp.

The Ute warrior continued riding boldly in front of the Kiowas, shouting his war cry. By sign language and loud whoops he made it clear to the Kiowas what he thought of them and of their ancestors. Glumly the Kiowas gazed at the bloody lance blade which the Ute flourished for them to see. None of them cared to redden that blade again. They thought of the white buffalo robe, and scowled at Bear Claw.

Bear Claw loosened his rein, and Gavilán shot forward, out toward the Ute on the black pony. Gavilán carried his head high, watching the enemy as he would a wild steer or a maddened buffalo bull. They circled and wheeled between the two war parties, while the Utes shrieked encouragement and the Kiowas watched in silence. When the black pony turned away at what the Ute thought was a safe distance, Gavilán dashed at him so quickly that Bear Claw nearly lost his seat. He recovered and found himself in the advantage. The Ute was fleeing, and could not use his weapons against any enemy coming from behind him.

As the two ponies thundered over the prairie Bear Claw raised his lance and cracked the Ute sharply across the shoulders. The Kiowas whooped for joy, while Bear Claw swung Gavilán and galloped back to rejoin his own party.

The Ute rejoicing ceased as the Utes saw their best warrior humiliated. It was worse than if he had been wounded or killed. Shouting a few farewell insults, the Utes turned and rode toward their own lands.

Emboldened by his success, Bear Claw planned a raid against the powerful Oglala tribe of the Sioux. Mounted on Gavilán, he rode through the Kiowa camp singing his war song. At his tepee the raiders assembled. They started out on foot to invade the lands of the dreaded Oglalas. If their luck held they would steal into an Oglala camp and ride home on good Oglala ponies.

Days passed before they returned in triumph, riding and driving some of the finest war ponies of the Oglalas. Bear Claw was now a famous warrior. The Great Spirit loved him, the Kiowas exclaimed, even though he no longer owned a white buffalo robe.

The Kiowa scouts were alert, for the Oglalas would surely seek revenge. This was as certain as snow in winter and hot sun in summer. Insult and vengeance had been the story between each tribe and its enemies for so long that no one had any idea who had started the disputes in the first place.

A small band of Oglalas was discovered one day near the edge of the Kiowa hunting grounds, and far away from any large Oglala camp. Oglala bands often wandered boldly over their vast hunting grounds in small groups, to hunt or to catch wild horses. Kiowa scouts watched the band at a safe distance. The Oglalas were tricky, and it might well be a trap.

After several days of watching the Kiowas grew bolder. The warriors met in the council lodge to plan their sudden attack. Ten warriors on swift ponies would charge through the little camp and drive off the pony herd. Other warriors would be ready nearby to hold back the Sioux while the raiders drove the ponies toward Kiowa country.

Bear Claw led the charge on the camp. As Gavilán raced over the prairie toward the Oglala tepees, Bear Claw heard Oglala war whoops. A large war party dashed toward the hidden Kiowas, while a smaller group of Oglalas rode to save the pony herd. The carefully planned Oglala trap was fast closing on the Kiowas.

The Kiowa warriors following Bear Claw turned their ponies toward their own lands and whipped them furiously. The Oglalas left the pony herd and raced to cut off the Kiowas' escape. Gavilán could carry him to safety easily, Bear Claw knew, but his companions might not escape at all unless he could slow up the Oglalas.

Whooping loudly he rode on toward the Oglala pony herd, waving his robe to stampede the ponies into a run. The Oglala warriors pulled up, let the fleeing Kiowas escape, and dashed back to save the herd. Bear Claw con-

tinued whooping and waving his robe, trying to scatter the ponies.

A glance told him his companions were safe, for they had stopped to wait for him. Driving the ponies, he crouched low over Gavilán's back, as Oglala arrows whined over his head. A warrior dashed in close and let fly an arrow. It caught Bear Claw in the shoulder.

Numbly he clung to his racing pony, while the Oglala tried to finish him off. His fingers lost their hold on Gavilán's mane, and he tumbled to the ground. Gavilán and the Oglala raced on. Two Kiowa warriors, riding side by side, galloped to where Bear Claw lay and picked him from the ground without slowing down. They carried him to safety before the Oglalas had gotten the frightened pony herd under control.

The warrior who had wounded Bear Claw rode into the herd and caught Gavilán's dragging rein. He led the buckskin out of the herd, while his comrades crowded around to admire his prize. Happily the Oglala warriors rode back to the main camp, satisfied with the revenge. Now it would be the Kiowa's turn.

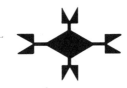

VI

ACROSS THE
MOUNTAINS

THE OGLALAS SOON MOVED into winter camp. Gray Eagle, who had captured Gavilán, led his new war pony on the long trip, keeping him ready in case enemies attacked the traveling band. The Oglalas crossed the Platte River and separated into small bands for the winter. Gray Eagle and his companions chose a sheltered valley where cottonwood trees grew profusely.

Before the snows fell the ponies were herded where they could graze on buffalo grass. When snow lay heavily over the ground, the women and boys brought cottonwood branches and bark to the war and buffalo ponies. Hungrily they chewed off the rich bark, while farther away the less fortunate pack ponies pawed at the crusted snow and gnawed each other's manes and tails.

One day they heard a distant rumble and roar. Gray Eagle and other Oglala warriors looked at one another, and burst into song. Gray Eagle swung to Gavilán's lean back and rode slowly down the valley toward the river. He drew up on the river bank, and watched the ice breaking up in the river, crumbling and crashing downstream with deafening noise. This was, for the Oglalas, the first sign of spring.

Soon the reasons for the Oglala warriors' songs of rejoicing appeared. Green shoots of grass pushed up through the withered stalks, and only a few patches of snow remained in shaded areas. The days grew warmer, and the ponies began to shed their shaggy coats of winter hair. The boys threw off their heavy winter robes. Warriors who before had been silent now talked of raids against the Pawnees and Kiowas and Cheyennes in the days to come, and of the Sun Dance.

One day the Dog Soldiers, the camp police, rode through the camp. "Prepare to move in the morning," they shouted. The women prepared their belongings for the move, throwing away anything they could get along without.

At daybreak the buffalo-hide tepees came down, and the women packed the willow baskets on the travois poles. The Dog Soldiers led the way down the valley. Gray Eagle rode an old pony and led Gavilán. They traveled slowly, for all of the ponies were still weak from the long winter. Once out of the valley they soon met other Oglala bands, and stopped to rest the ponies, and to exchange news.

Day after day other bands joined them, until the whole Oglala tribe was reunited. As the grass grew taller,

Gavilán and the other ponies recovered their strength rapidly. The gaunt ribs and backbones were soon covered by layers of muscle and fat. The heavy winter coats were gone, and the ponies were covered with short, shiny hair.

Herds of buffalo moving north from Comanche country flowed over the plains. The Oglala warriors mounted their best ponies and raced after the buffaloes. After every hunt there was feasting on hump ribs and tongue and liver, until they forgot the long winter, the endless days of hunger.

Other Sioux tribes now joined the Oglalas, until the Brulés, Hunkpapas, Sans Arcs and Two Kettles were assembled for the Sun Dance. The tepees were set up in a huge circle, each tribe remaining together in one part of the circle.

Gray Eagle was silent as the tribes gathered. When he spoke, it was only of the Sun Dance, when he and a few other brave young men would prove their courage to all the Sioux. He thought of the final stage of the dance, and hoped his courage would hold. That was when old warriors cut slits in the chest muscles of the dancers, and tied them by rawhide thongs to the pole. Each dancer had to tear himself loose.

Before the Sun Dance began, each of the dancers had to give away everything he owned, for no one who would be a great warrior could show any sentimental attachment to any possession, even to his favorite war pony. Generosity, too, was a sign of greatness, and the more valuable the gift, the greater the warrior. Each dancer was given bits of wood, which he threw into the huge crowd. "Whoever catches this gets my buckskin pony," said Gray Eagle, and flung the wood away.

A young warrior leaped high in the air and caught it. Leaving the crowd at once, he ran to Gray Eagle's tepee, untied Gavilán, and led him away. He tied the pony near an old, weather-beaten lodge in another part of the camp, among the Hunkpapas.

The Sun Dance continued day and night for three days. Warriors, women and children came and went, watching the dancers, then joining friends for feasts on buffalo hump ribs and liver, eating far into the night until they could do no more than fling themselves on their robes and sleep. No scouts were sent out, and no raiders left camp, for the Sun Dance was a time of celebration only, the time when young Sioux warriors proved to all that the tribe would have brave men to protect it in the future.

No one was worried about enemies, for when all the Teton Sioux tribes were assembled, they outnumbered any of their enemies. With people coming and going at any time of the day or night, the camp was in complete confusion. No one noticed a little group of strange warriors steal in among the tepees not long after midnight on the third day of the Sun Dance.

The strange warriors waited until the camp was fairly quiet, until the Sioux warriors had stopped singing their songs and had flung themselves on their robes. Quietly the strangers selected the ponies they wanted and led them slowly out of the silent camp. One of them led Gavilán.

Once out of hearing of the Sioux, they mounted and rode hard toward the western mountains, not stopping except for brief rests and to listen for pursuers. Up the mountainside they went, following a narrow trail toward

the pass at the summit. They crossed one range and followed the path down into the valley and up the opposite side.

When at last the weary ponies carried them out of the mountains into the Great Basin country, the warriors stopped. They were safe now, for the Sioux would not pursue them so far. While the ponies rested, the Nez Percé warriors hunted and talked of their good fortune, of their revenge on the hated Sioux.

They continued on, crossing the basin to the mountains beyond, and soon had rejoined their tribe. The Nez Percés had many ponies, and wanted those of the Sioux only to humiliate their enemies. Their favorite color was roan with dark spots on the rump, the type known as Appaloosa. There were in their herds, however, ponies of all colors, and some, like Gavilán, bearing Spanish brands.

Gavilán had become rested and had recovered his strength by the time strangers rode up to the Nez Percé camp. They were a band of white men and one Indian woman, soldiers who were coming from farther to the west. The white men camped near the Nez Percés, and several came to talk to the chief.

"Captain Clark would like to trade for ponies," one of the soldiers told the chief through an interpreter. "Will you ask your warriors to bring us any ponies they want to trade? We have been to the ocean, and we're on our way home now, to report to the Great Father in Washington."

The chief agreed. Next morning the Nez Percé warriors brought their ponies to the camp of Lewis and Clark, who were now completing their survey of Louisiana territory for President Jefferson. The warrior who had stolen Gavilán from the Sioux brought him to trade, for he had many ponies. What he wanted was a musket like those of the white soldiers, a skinning knife, and an ax for his wife.

The bargaining began. The warrior held out for the things he wanted, but the captains refused to pay so much for an Indian pony when other warriors were more reasonable. "When we get to the Mississippi we'll trade them or turn them loose," Captain Lewis said. "All we need is enough to get us there. They don't have to be the best."

Finally a young soldier took Gavilán's rein from the

Nez Percé warrior and rode the buckskin pony around the camp. When he returned, he spoke quietly to Captain Lewis. The captain nodded his head. The soldier went to his own tent and returned with a musket, a knife and an ax, which he handed to the Nez Percé warrior. He tied Gavilán with the other ponies and called to his companions. They came to look.

"This is the best pony I'll ever own," he said.

One of the soldiers shook his head. "Maybe so," he said. "But Indian ponies are all alike, Dave. Few of them are really fast, but they're tough and mean, and they'll run till they drop dead. This one looks pretty good, but he's still just an Indian pony, not worth any more than any other one."

"I rode him a little," Dave replied. "He's got plenty of speed, and I'll bet he can keep going as long as any horse alive. And he isn't an Indian pony." He pointed to the Sombrero brand on Gavilán's left hip.

Next day the soldiers broke camp and crossed the mountains north of the pass where the Nez Percés had fled from the Sioux. "This is Blackfoot country," the guide warned them. "They're the meanest varmints on the plains. They love a good scrap, and they're not afraid of guns. Watch out! Any man who's careless won't keep his hair long in Blackfoot country."

VII

▶▶▶▶▶▶▶▶▶▶▶▶

LEWIS AND CLARK

THE SOLDIERS RODE CAUTIOUSLY through the Blackfoot country. Lewis and Clark made notes on everything they saw—on the streams they crossed, the mountains, the wild animals, the trees and wild flowers.

"We haven't seen an Indian yet," said Sergeant Gass on the third day. "I thought this country was supposed to be crawling with Blackfeet."

The soldiers grunted in reply. "There's plenty of Indian sign if you look for it," said Dave. He nodded his head toward a broken twig near the trail, then pointed to a slender spiral of smoke, barely visible against the haze of the mountains. "My buckskin pony's been sniffing the breeze every time it comes up. We may not have seen them, but I'll bet the Blackfeet have seen us, and are looking at us right now."

The force split up, to explore the country more widely. Lewis and Clark were clearly worried about Blackfeet, but they also knew that President Jefferson would question them about every bit of the country in the West, and they would have to know the answers. Dave and four others were sent on a swing through the country to the north to chart the rivers and streams; this was the country where Dave had seen the smoke signal.

"Watch out for the Blackfeet," Captain Lewis warned them. "Keep out of trouble. We'll meet you down on the Upper Missouri in about a week, if all goes well. That's about 250 miles from here, as I figure it. Get your notes and come as soon as you can."

Dave and the others mounted and rode off. For two days they rode through rough country, past small herds of buffaloes. They watched carefully for signs of Blackfeet, but except for frequent pony tracks and distant smoke signals there was little indication that enemies were near. The fact that the buffaloes were grazing quietly was at least a sign that the Blackfeet were not hunting them.

When they made camp the third night, Gavilán stamped impatiently at his tether, and snorted. Dave came to him. "What's the matter, Buck?" he asked. "Indians?" Gavilán looked out into the darkness, ears pointing forward. Dave hurried to the sergeant. An alert guard watched the ponies through the night, while the others slept.

At daybreak Blackfoot warriors rode up to the edge of the camp, bows strung, long-bladed lances lying across their ponies' shoulders. The soldiers were ready for them, and, at a signal from the sergeant, cocked their muskets and swung them carelessly in the direction of the Blackfeet. There were twenty warriors and only five soldiers. The sergeant and the chief talked to one another in sign language. Dave and the others watched the stern warriors, aware that they were not impressed by what the sergeant was telling them. It seemed clear that the Blackfeet were determined to fight, and that some of them, at least, planned to ride into camp with scalps hanging from their lances.

"Tell them they might as well go home, Sarge," Dave said. "We don't have half enough scalps to go around."

"We're in for real trouble, boys," the sergeant said quietly. "Dave, you saddle all the ponies. Make it quick, but try not to act like you're in a hurry. Any little thing can start them off. And if we have to run for it, watch out for those lances!"

With the Blackfeet only thirty paces away, Dave turned his back and began saddling the ponies, hoping that someone would warn him in time if an arrow headed toward his back. He saddled Gavilán first and dropped the reins. The well-trained horse stood impatiently at his side, tossing his head and looking toward the fierce Blackfeet while Dave threw the saddles on the other ponies. Dave looked again at the Blackfeet as he drew the last cinch tight. They were getting restless, but they were still not eager to start the attack while four guns were trained on them. They knew well enough that four men would die immediately, and no four of them cared to be the first. But it was clear to Dave that they would not wait much longer, that soon one of them would decide to be a hero. Before any of the soldiers could reload, they would be riddled with arrows.

Dave released the hammer of his musket quietly, so the click was barely audible, and slid it into its saddle case. The sergeant heard it, and glanced at him as he swung into the saddle.

"I didn't order you to mount up, son," said the sergeant softly. "We'll all go together, or none of us will make it. It's our only chance."

We haven't any chance, sergeant," Dave replied. "Once they attack we're all done for. I'm going to take them on a little ride. You all best get back to the others as quick as you can. I'll meet you there if all goes well."

While the sergeant shouted for him to wait, Dave swung Gavilán around. Whooping loudly, he galloped away, crouching low over the buckskin's neck as arrows whistled over him. The Blackfeet shrieked their war cries and whipped their ponies after him.

Gavilán ran with a long, effortless stride, easily keeping out of range of the Blackfoot arrows. The little Blackfoot ponies sprinted madly after him, while the warriors whooped encouragement to one another. Dave glanced back just once and saw his companions galloping off to the south. He held Gavilán back, so the Blackfeet would not give up the chase and turn after the soldiers.

He breathed heavily as he rode, for the Blackfeet seemed determined to lift his scalp no matter how long they had to follow him. He wondered why he was trying to be a hero, but he knew it was the only chance he or his friends had of escaping. He had no choice.

"Get me out of this, Buck," he breathed toward Gavilán's black-tipped ears, "and I'll either pasture you for life or turn you loose with the wild ones. That's what you really want, isn't it?"

Gavilán galloped on, his hard black hoofs drumming steadily over the ground. All day they rode. The country was strange to both Dave and Gavilán, but the horse picked his way through it, swinging up long valleys and across low hills. He skirted small bands of buffaloes, and sent frightened antelope sprinting to safety. At times he raised his head, pointing his ears forward, watching for other Blackfeet.

Behind them the angry Blackfeet came on, quiet now, but swinging their whips in determination and holding their deadly lances high, waiting for Gavilán to falter. They still showed no sign of giving up the chase. A single rider in their wild land could not possibly escape them if they kept on his trail long enough. Surely one of their ponies would outlast his. It was simply a question of which of them would be in on the kill when the soldier's pony gave out.

Darkness fell. Gavilán's shiny hide was dark with sweat, except where foamy lather clung to his flanks. On through the night he ran, until Dave pulled him up, sides heaving, to listen for pursuers. Far behind him he heard the click of ponies' hoofs over loose stones. He let Gavilán walk on, guiding him toward the south and east, where he would find Lewis and Clark.

All night they kept on, Dave half dozing wearily in the saddle while Gavilán picked his way through the Blackfoot country, splashing through streams and struggling up steep hills beyond. He cocked an ear backward occasionally, and heard the Blackfoot ponies. When they seemed to be coming too close, he trotted or loped, keeping well ahead of them. At such times Dave patted him on the neck. "Good boy," he mumbled. "Good boy."

At daybreak Dave groaned, rubbed his reddened eyes, and pulled Gavilán to a halt. He heard the pursuing Blackfeet, and let his weary pony trot ahead. When the Indians came into sight he saw that some must have abandoned the chase, for there were only ten warriors left.

All day long Gavilán kept on, though the chase had slowed down. When the warriors came too close, he swung into a lope, and trotted or walked when they slowed down. By late afternnon there were only five pursuers left in sight. At dark they were still doggedly following. Dave licked his dry, swollen lips, and wondered how much longer he could hold out.

Gavilán wandered wearily on through the night, while Dave sagged in the saddle, less awake than asleep. Somehow he kept from falling to the ground, though his muscles ached. At daybreak he turned stiffly in the saddle and strained his bloodshot eyes. There were no Blackfeet in sight.

"I'd get off and let you rest," he told Gavilán, "only I'd never be able to get on again. We'd better keep moving a little longer. Shouldn't be far to the camp now."

Behind him he saw a smoke signal rising, and knew

that the tiny puffs of smoke were warnings to other Blackfoot bands to watch for him. His head sagged as he rode on, letting Gavilán choose his way, too exhausted to care much whether the Blackfeet killed him or not. If fresh bands found him, he would not even be able to put up a fight.

Gavilán walked on, head low. When they crossed a stream, he stopped at the edge and drank deeply. In the afternoon he pricked up his ears and sniffed the breeze. Whinnying weakly, he began to trot. When he stopped at the soldiers' camp, Dave slid weakly to the ground. Soldiers gathered around him.

"The others will be along soon as they can," he mumbled. "We had trouble with Blackfeet. Buck and I had to take a shortcut, so they'd leave the others alone."

They stretched him out on a blanket. "Look after my horse," he said, and fell asleep.

Quickly the soldiers unsaddled Gavilán, removed the bridle, and rubbed him dry. They tied him where grass was thick, and carried water to him in their hats. He nibbled weakly at the grass, then slept.

They camped there for four days before Dave could ride again. The sergeant and the three soldiers he had left behind arrived the second day. "I don't know how you got here so quick," the sergeant said to Dave. "That was at least 150 miles as the crow flies, and no telling where-all you went." Dave smiled, and went back to sleep.

On the fifth day they mounted Dave on an extra pony, and led Gavilán.

"He's in better shape than you are, Dave," said the sergeant. "How did you ever get away from them, anyway? We thought that crazy stunt of yours would be your last, even if it saved all of us. I've been trying to figure out what I'd write your parents about you."

Dave smiled weakly. "It was easy enough," he said. "I just promised old Buck I'd turn him loose to run with the wild ones first chance I had, and he did the rest. All I had to do was to hang on, and that was hard enough after the first day."

The soldiers laughed at Dave's joke. "Turn loose a pony that can run like that? A likely story." Dave's smile faded.

The soldiers rode on, through Sioux country, and down across the prairies along the muddy Platte. When they reached the Mississippi, it was time to sell the ponies and board canoes. John Colter turned to Dave as the canoes were being loaded.

"I've been paid off," he said. "I aim to stay out here and trap beaver. I want to buy that buckskin pony of yours. I'll pay you what any two ponies are worth for him, and I reckon he'll be cheap at that."

Dave was standing by Gavilán's side, unsaddling him, and fighting down a lump which kept rising in his throat. He was not able to answer for a moment, so he threw the saddle on the ground and slipped off the bridle. Gavilán stood there, looking at him.

"I swore I'd turn him loose, John, if he got me out of that scrape with the Blackfeet. He may not know it, but I do." He slapped Gavilán on the rump, and drove him toward the open prairie.

"Get on your way, Buck," he shouted. "I can't take you with me, and no one else is going to ride you if I can help it. Get!"

Gavilán shook his head and galloped out onto the prairie. Gradually he swung to the southward. Far out on the prairie he stopped to look back for a moment. Dave still stood near the river, motionless, watching him. Shaking his head so his black mane flew, Gavilán trotted on. Free!

VIII

SOMBRERO RANCH

WINTER OVERTOOK GAVILÁN ON THE PLAINS, near the Paw-nee country. He joined a band of young stallions. They grazed peacefully through the winter, pawing through the snow for grass and gnawing the bark of cottonwood trees in sheltered valleys. Gavilán remembered the mes-quite thickets and strong sun on the range where he was born.

The winter was long and severe. Once prairie wolves attacked the wild stallions. They stood, heads together, heels flying. For hours the hungry wolves circled about them, snapping at their hind legs, trying to sever the ten-dons. Finally the wolves limped away, defeated.

When spring came and the snow melted, the gaunt stal-lions began shedding their heavy winter coats. Quickly they put on flesh as new grass appeared, and soon all were strong again. Other herds of wild horses came out of winter hiding, herds of mares and yearling colts, fiercely guarded by jealous stallions.

The young stallions scattered over the plains, each looking for a herd of mares of his own. Gavilán grazed on toward the southwest, entering the ranges of other herds. From a distance the stallions trumpeted warnings and challenges.

In the Comanche country he came to a herd of mares and stopped. His strength was now fully recovered. Neck arched, he whinnied at the mares, and they raised their heads to look. The ground shook as a powerful black stallion galloped toward him, to stand between him and the mares.

Gavilán advanced at a trot, while the black squealed with rage, laid his ears back, and bared his teeth. On his neck and shoulders were patches of white hair, where he

had been wounded in other battles defending his herd. As Gavilán approached the black stallion charged.

They struck shoulder to shoulder, both reeling from the terrific impact, then recovering instantly. Rearing, they struck out with their front hoofs, snapping at each other, while the mares watched to see which would be the victor. They lunged together again, teeth clicking at each other's throat. Their eyes were red with rage, and their breath came in gasps. Teeth closed on bits of skin. Furiously they fought, neither giving ground.

Long and hard they battled, but in the end there was no victor, no loser. Both staggered away, the black stallion to his herd, Gavilán to a shady valley where he could rest.

For three days he remained among the alders and willows, switching at flies to keep them from his wounds. He did not wait until the cuts were completely healed. When he was fully rested, he trotted out to find the black stallion and his herd, to win it for himself.

The herd had ranged far since the fight, but Gavilán followed the trail, sniffing the stallion's tracks. He trumpeted a challenge, and once more the black came out to defend his herd. Recognizing Gavilán, he came more slowly this time. He wanted no fight if it could be avoided, but he was ready to battle again if Gavilán approached his herd. As the two splendid animals charged each other, the mares stopped grazing once more to watch the battle.

Furiously Gavilán threw his shoulder into the black's side, knocking him off balance. Wheeling instantly, he

lashed out with both hind hoofs, catching the black full on the ribs and knocking the breath out of him. The black grunted in pain and staggered a few steps. Before he could recover, Gavilán struck him in the side with his powerful shoulders, knocking him to the ground. The black scrambled to his feet as Gavilán came at him again, and galloped away. His will to fight was gone.

Proudly Gavilán trotted to the herd of mares, whinnying shrilly. One by one they gathered about him, touching noses with him in greeting. Then they went on grazing, satisfied with the new ruler of the herd.

The black stallion returned a few days later and fought desperately to recover his herd. Gavilán drove him off again and again, and finally he gave up. As Gavilán began driving the herd southward he looked back. The black stood at the crest of a hill, whinnying to the mares. They ignored him.

During the summer, after the new colts were born, Gavilán moved his herd farther south through Comanche country, toward northern New Mexico. The mares were reluctant to leave their old range, and a few attempted to turn back. Laying back his ears, Gavilán nipped at them. They went on, knowing they could not escape.

Comanche warriors saw the herd and recognized Gavilán by his color and his Sombrero brand. Twisted Horn's famous war pony was back! They sent a rider after the herd, and scattered relays of riders around the range, to run the herd down. Knowing that wild horses always stayed in their familiar territory, they were sure they could run the herd down by keeping riders after it day and night.

The Comanche warrior followed the herd until his pony gave out, but no other rider appeared to take his place. Gavilán had kept between him and the mares and colts, driving them ever to the south, away from the range where the relays of Comanche riders waited. The puzzled Comanches gave up; the wild herd was obviously abandoning its range. There was no hope of running it down.

Each day, as the herd wandered south, the land became more familiar to Gavilán. Head held high, he pranced along after the mares and colts, almost floating over the ground. Now he was in the land he had remembered during the long winters on the northern plains.

Early one morning, after they had crossed the Pecos,

he drove the mares over a familiar hill. There below them lay the ranch house and corrals. The mares snorted a little from fright, but the young colts galloped about without scenting any danger. Gavilán moved the herd nearer to the corrals, and stood there, neck arched, staring at the house.

A tall young man came out of the ranch house, glanced at the rising sun, stretched, and yawned. The breeze carried an old familiar scent to Gavilán.

Gavilán's piercing whinny echoed through the little valley. Alfredo looked up in surprise, then ran toward the corral. Gavilán walked to meet him, nickering softly. Alfredo threw his arms around the golden neck and buried his face in the black mane.

"Gavilán!" he said, and his voice sounded strange, as if he were choking. "Gavilán! I knew you'd come back some day. You're home now, and no one but me will ever ride you again."

He patted Gavilán's neck and back, examining the patches of white hair where the skin had been broken by Bent Bow's lance and in the battles with the black stallion. He gave Gavilán a friendly slap on the rump and watched him trot back to the mares. As the herd grazed slowly out toward the Sombrero range, Alfredo stood by the corral, watching.